Emmy
the Exaggerating
Elephant

Fenton
the Fearful Frog

Gertie
the Grungy Goat

Herbie
the Happy
Hamster

Ivy
the Impatient
Iguana

Ollie
the Obedient
Ostrich

Perry
the Polite
Porcupine

Queenie
the Quiet Quail

Rupert
the Resourceful
Rhinoceros

Wendy
the Wise
Woodchuck

Xavier
the X-ploring
Xenops

Yori
the Yucky Yak

Ziggy
the Zippy Zebra

NOTE TO PARENTS

Sylvester and the Sand Castle
A story about sportsmanship and fairness

In this story, Sylvester the Stubborn Squirrel misses out on a lot of fun because he insists on having his way. By setting a good example, his AlphaPet friends help him realize the advantages of being adaptable and open-minded.

In addition to enjoying this story with your child, you can use it to teach a gentle lesson about the importance of being a good sport and cooperating with others.

You can also use this story to introduce the letter S. As you read about Sylvester the Stubborn Squirrel, ask your child to listen for all the words that start with S and point to the objects that begin with S. When you've finished reading the story, your child will enjoy doing the activity at the end of the book.

The AlphaPets™ characters were conceived and created by Ruth Lerner Perle.
Characters interpreted and designed by Deborah Colvin Borgo.
Cover/book design and production by Norton & Company.
Logo design by Deborah Colvin Borgo and Nancy S. Norton.
Printed and Manufactured in the United States of America

Sylvester and the Sand Castle

RUTH LERNER PERLE

Illustrated by Richard Max Kolding

Grolier Enterprises Inc.,   Danbury, Connecticut

One hot summer Sunday, some of the AlphaPets decided to go to the beach. Sylvester the Stubborn Squirrel was standing on the corner waiting for Vinnie the Vocal Vulture to pick him up.

Before long, Sylvester saw Vinnie driving down the street. Perry the Polite Porcupine, Katy the Kind Koala, Lizzy the Lazy Lamb, and Fenton the Fearful Frog were already in the car with him.

"Good morning, good morning, Sylvester!" Vinnie called. "Hop in the back! There's plenty of room in the middle."

"The middle!" cried Sylvester. "I'm not getting in any middle seat. If I have to sit there, I'm not going."

"Come on, Sylvester," Perry said. "Try to be fair. *Nobody* likes to sit in the middle. That's why we always take turns, and today it's your turn."

"I don't care," Sylvester said, and he started to leave.

"You can take my seat, Sylvester," Katy said. "Get in, and let's have a good time."

So Sylvester took Katy's seat and they drove off.

When they arrived at the beach, Perry asked, "Shall we sit near the water or on the sand dunes?"

"Makes no difference to me," Fenton said. "As long as I'm safe from the sand . . . and sun . . . and sea."

"It's the sandy sand dunes for me!" said Vinnie. "Let's sit in the dunes!"

"Good idea," agreed Lizzy. "It's more relaxing in the sand dunes."

"No sand dunes for me. Oh, no!" Sylvester declared. "When I'm at the beach I like to be near the water and I won't sit anywhere else."

"Well, all right, if it's that important to you, my friend," Vinnie said. "I'm sure we'll all enjoy the waterside just as well." Everyone agreed and they walked down to the waterfront.

The AlphaPets spread out their blankets near the edge of the water. After everybody sat down, Fenton put on his sun hat, socks, and sunglasses. Then he gave everyone a little tube of sunscreen.

"Too much sun is dangerous," he said. "This sunscreen will protect our skin from getting burned."

"Not me! I don't need that sunscreen!" Sylvester yelled.

"But your nose is getting red already," Katy said.

"How can you say that? I *never* burn. Never!" Sylvester insisted. "No sunscreen for me, definitely not."

Katy opened her picnic basket and took out a bag of assorted sandwiches. She offered some to her friends.

"I get to pick a sandwich first!" Sylvester said, pushing his way ahead of Fenton and Perry.

"Please, Sylvester! Wait your turn," Perry said.

Sylvester crossed his arms in front of his chest. "If I don't get to choose a sandwich first, I won't eat at all!" he declared.

So Perry very politely let Sylvester choose first.

Vinnie opened his lunch box and offered everybody slices of ripe avocado.

"What's an avocado?" Sylvester wanted to know. "I never saw one of those before."

"Try it, it's delicious!" Lizzy said.

"Oh, no! Not me! That stuff looks slimy and it's green. I never eat anything that's green," Sylvester announced.

"Why don't you just try a bite?" Perry suggested. "You might like it."

"Uh uh, not me." Sylvester insisted. He unwrapped his sandwich and started to eat.

When they were all finished eating, Vinnie said, "Let's build a sand castle!"

"Good idea!" Fenton agreed. "But first let's put on a little more sunscreen. The sun is really strong today."

So, everyone put on more sunscreen—everyone except Sylvester.

"Your cheeks and forehead are turning bright red," said Fenton, offering him the sunscreen. But Sylvester still refused it. "I never burn," he insisted. "Never."

"Okay," Vinnie said. "Now let's start building our castle. Perry and I will dig a moat and pile up sand for towers. Katy, you and Lizzy can collect seashells and stones for decorations. Sylvester and Fenton can bring pails of water."

"I don't want to bring the water. I want to dig the moat," Sylvester declared.

By now Vinnie was getting tired of Sylvester's stubborn ways.

"Well, you can't always have it your way," Vinnie said. "Sometimes you have to take turns and be considerate of what others want to do."

Sylvester stamped his feet and kicked at the sand. "I want to dig the moat! I want to dig the moat!" he cried.

"Well, I'm afraid you're not going to get your way this time!" Perry said.

"Then I'm not playing with you!" Sylvester screamed. He threw down his pail and stomped off by himself.

The AlphaPets decided to leave Sylvester alone and started to work together happily.

They dug deep holes
and trenches . . .

collected shells,
seaweed, sticks,
and stones . . .

carried buckets
of water . . .

and piled up
a mountain
of sand.

Sylvester could hear the AlphaPets joking and having a good time. He wanted to join them, but instead he dug his heels into the sand and stared at the sea.

"Why won't they let me dig the moat?" he muttered under his breath. "Why can't I have things my way?"

Sylvester was feeling sad and angry. He was also getting hot and thirsty, and his shoulders were starting to burn.

Before long, the sand castle was almost finished.
Sylvester watched as Vinnie planted a flag at the top
of the castle.

"That looks like fun. I wish I could play," he thought
to himself. But he just sat and stared.

"What this castle needs is a big wall all around it," Perry said.

"That's a great idea," Lizzy agreed. "But I think it's too much work for just the five of us. Six people would be just right." Everyone stopped and looked at Sylvester.

Katy called over to Sylvester. "How about helping us?"

At first Sylvester pretended not to hear them.

"Sylvester! Come and help us!" they all called.

"Well, maybe," Sylvester said.

But as he started to get up, he screamed. "*YEOW! OUCH!* My shoulders! My back! My arms!"

"Oh, my word! Looks like you really have a bad sunburn!" Vinnie said, shaking his head.

Fenton ran for his first aid kit and the AlphaPets put ointment on Sylvester's burn. Then Fenton reached into his bag and gave Sylvester an extra hat and shirt that he had in his bag—just in case of an emergency.

The cooling ointment felt good. "Er . . . ah . . . thank you. I guess I should have used the sunscreen after all," Sylvester said. "But now I feel much better, so let's build that wall!"

Everybody worked together, digging, carrying water, and patting the sand.

"Hmmm . . . this is really fun," Sylvester thought. "I should have joined in sooner."

Soon the wall was finished. Everybody admired the beautiful job they had done.

Vinnie poured some sarsaparilla sodas for all the builders. Then he got up to make a speech.

"Ahem, ahem," he started. "I would like to dedicate this most magnificent medieval structure to friendship and cooperation. Without those two ingredients, this castle would not have come to be. No indeed! Not at all. If I said it once, I said it a hundred . . . no, a thousand times. Yes, a thousand times: The secret of getting a big job done is team work. Yes, my friends, team work! Working together to achieve a common goal!"

Vinnie put his arm around Sylvester and offered him a cup of soda. "Here's some nice cool sarsaparilla," he said with a smile. "Let's all drink to friendship and cooperation."

Sylvester started to say that he would never try a drink that has so many sss's in it. But instead, he took the cup and had a little sip.

"Hmmm," Sylvester said with a happy smile. "This stuff doesn't taste too bad. Not bad at all."

Let's learn these words together.

six

sand castle

socks

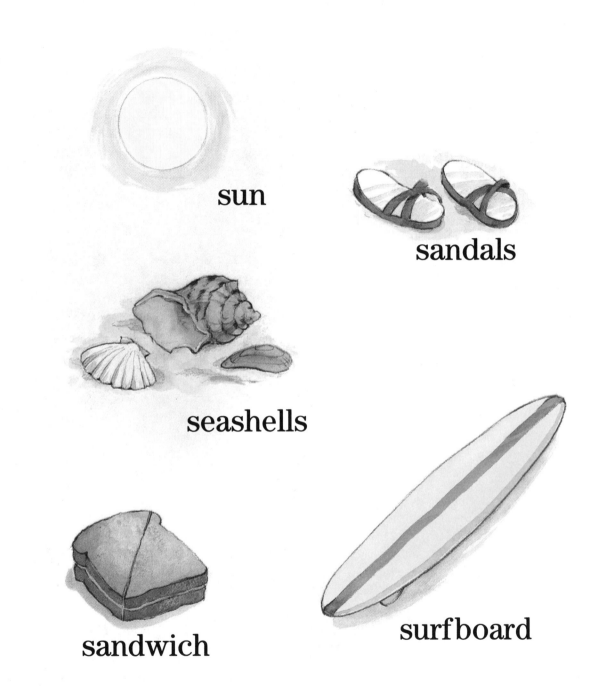

sun

sandals

seashells

sandwich

surfboard

Look back at the pages of this book and try to find these and other words that start with S.

Aa Bb

Gg Hh

Mm Nn Oo Pp

Uu Vv Ww